THE PHANTOM OF THE OPERA

Introduction

Gaston Leroux was born in 1868 in Paris, France, into a very wealthy family. After studying law, he inherited a million francs – and he spent it all very quickly! So he had to work for a living. Leroux started to write for a newspaper in Paris. By the age of thirty, he was a full-time writer of mystery and detective novels.

Gaston Leroux became well known in 1907 for The *Mystery of the Yellow Room*, a novel that introduced a teenage crime reporter. Two years later, he wrote *The Phantom of the Opera*, his best-known book today.

The Phantom of the Opera is spine chilling and full of drama, just like a real opera. The phantom of the title – which frightens everyone with his deformed face – lives beneath the Paris Opera House where he becomes obsessed with a young singer, called Christine Daaé. As he enchants her more and more with his music, she begins to wonder whether he really is a phantom. The building that Leroux described actually exists – and it does have enormous cellars with an underground lake.

Many films have been made of this story. In 1987, Andrew Lloyd Webber produced *The Phantom of the Opera* as a musical.

Gaston Leroux died in 1927 at the age of fifty-nine.

CHAPTER ONE

A New Singer

A new singer had just given a wonderful performance at the Paris Opera House. Her name was Christine Daaé. At the last minute, she had replaced Carlotta, who was ill, as Margarita in an opera called Faust. Nobody had ever heard a voice like hers. The audience went mad with delight and clapped until Christine was carried from the stage weeping and fainting.

In his box overlooking the stage, the Count de Chagny applauded loudly, too. He was a handsome man of forty-one and the head of one of the most distinguished families in France. His younger brother Raoul sat next to him, his face pale with surprise.

"I wonder if Christine will remember me?" Raoul thought. "We used to play on the beach together when we were children. I must go back-stage to meet her."

As he made his way to Christine Daaé's dressing room, Raoul passed some of the ballet dancers in the narrow corridors. They were talking about a phantom which had been haunting the Opera House for some time: how he seemed to appear from nowhere in the shape of a gentleman wearing a black evening suit – and how he vanished as soon as he was seen.

Joseph Buquet, a scene-shifter, had met him once on the staircase leading to the cellars. "His skin is yellow and so tightly stretched over his bones that it looks like the face of a dead person," he told everybody afterwards. "His eyes are so deep that they look like two big black holes. His nose is small and he hardly has any hair. Ugh!"

Now Raoul de Chagny entered Christine Daaé's dressing room just as she was opening her eyes. "Monsieur," she whispered. "Who are you?"

Raoul kissed her hand. "Don't you remember?" he asked. "I am the little boy who went into the sea to rescue your scarf when the wind blew it away. I should like to speak to you in private, Mademoiselle Christine."

"No," she replied. "Go away! I wish to be alone."

Raoul waited impatiently outside her door. To his surprise, he heard a man's voice coming from the dressing room. "Christine, you must love me!" he said. And Christine's trembling voice replied, "How can you talk like that, when I sing only for you! Tonight I gave you my soul."

Raoul heard no more. He crept into a dark corner, his heart beating wildly, and waited for the man to leave. He knew that he loved Christine Daaé and he hated that man inside her room.

At last, Christine came out, but she did not see Raoul. When she had gone, he went into her dressing room. The gaslight had been turned out. He stood there in complete darkness.

"Why are you hiding?" Raoul called out, striking a match. "If you don't answer, you are a coward!"

The match lit up the room – but it was empty.

Raoul waited for ten minutes. Then he decided to leave. As he went through the door, an icy blast struck him in the face. He walked through the corridors for some time, not knowing where he was going. Suddenly, near the bottom of a staircase, he had to make way for a group of men carrying a stretcher. The person on it was covered with a white sheet.

"Who is that?" he asked.

"Joseph Buquet," one of the men answered. "He was found dead behind the scenery in the third cellar."

CHAPTER TWO

The Angel of Music

Christine Daaé did not continue her triumph at the Opera House. After that evening, she refused to sing again. She seemed afraid of her new success.

Raoul wrote to her many times, asking to meet her. At last, she sent him this note:

Monsieur:
I have not forgotten you, the little boy who rescued my scarf. Tomorrow is the anniversary of the death of my poor father, whom you knew. He is buried in Perros and I am going there to visit his grave. Christine Daaé.

Why had she written to him? Did she want him to follow her? Raoul dressed quickly and hurried to the railway station. On the long train journey to Perros, a town on the north coast of France, he thought about Christine all the time. He knew that he was in love with her.

Christine Daaé came from Sweden. Her father was a poor peasant, but he played the violin better than anybody else. One day, as he was playing at a fair – and Christine was singing – a Professor Valerius heard them. It was he who brought them both to France and paid for Christine's musical education. Like Raoul, they spent each summer by the sea in Perros.

As a young boy, Raoul loved listening to the stories that Christine's father knew so well.

"Every great musician receives a visit from the Angel of Music, at least once in his or her life," he used to tell them. "No one ever sees the Angel, but they remember its voice all their lives." He looked at Christine. "When I am in heaven, child, I shall send him to you."

Three years later, the old man had died.

In Perros, Raoul found Christine at the inn. She showed no surprise when he appeared.

"So you have come," she said quietly. "I knew that you would."

"Yes," Raoul replied. "You must realise that I love you, Christine, and I cannot live without you."

Christine blushed and turned away her head. "Me?" she asked. "You are dreaming, my friend." Then she burst out laughing. "Perhaps I was wrong to write to you," she said, "but seeing you at the Opera House reminded me of happy times long past."

"Do not laugh at me, Christine," Raoul said. "Why do you treat me in this way?"

Christine did not reply.

"I think I know the answer," Raoul said. "There was a

man in your dressing room that evening, someone to whom you said: "I sing only for you!" And he said: "Christine, you must love me!"'"

At these words, Christine turned pale. She staggered and seemed on the point of fainting. Two tears trickled down her cheeks. Then she ran to her room. Raoul did not know what to do. At last, he decided to visit her father's grave, too. As he stood there, Christine came to join him.

"Listen, Raoul," she said. "I am going to tell you something very serious. Do you remember the legend of the Angel of Music?"

"Of course I do," Raoul replied. "Your father first told it to me here in Perros."

"The Angel of Music has visited me," Christine said.

"I have no doubt of it," he replied. "No human being can sing as you sang the other evening. It was a miracle. No professor could teach you. Yes, you have heard the Angel of Music, Christine."

"He comes to my dressing-room," she said. "That is where I hear him. That is where you heard him."

Raoul laughed. "I think that somebody is playing a joke on you, Christine."

Christine gave a cry and ran from him. Raoul did not see her again until that evening – at half past eleven he saw her leave her room and go downstairs. He followed her to the churchyard.

"I want her to turn round to see me," he thought, "but she does not seem to hear me, although my footsteps are noisy on the hard snow."

Christine knelt down by her father's grave and prayed. As the church clock struck midnight, she looked up at the sky and stretched out her arms. Raoul heard the sound of violin music, music that her father had played to them as children. Then she got up and walked away.

As Raoul turned to follow her again, he saw a shadow gliding into the church door. He caught hold of the edge of its cloak. Just then, the moon shone through the window above the altar. The shadow turned round. Raoul saw a man with a face partly covered by a mask. He shuddered as its eyes looked straight at him.

He felt as if he were face to face with the devil!

CHAPTER THREE

Box Five

There were new managers at the Opera House, a Monsieur Richard and a Monsieur Moncharmin. They were delighted with their new jobs, so delighted that they forgot all about the rumours of a phantom – until the day they received a letter from him.

"Dear Managers," they read, "I have arrived at the Opera recently to find my box – Box Five – sold to somebody else. The previous managers were always kind to me. If you wish to live in peace, do not take away my box.

The Phantom of the Opera."

"This joke is not very funny," they said. "We shall sell tickets as usual to the public tonight for Box Five."

The following day, reports reached them of the rowdiness in Box Five during the performance, so noisy that the police had to be called. The managers sent for Madame Giry, who looked after the box.

"What happened last night?" Monsieur Richard demanded.

"The phantom was annoyed because you let his box!" she explained. "The managers before you never believed in him either, until he sent them tumbling down the stairs when they sat in his box. Since then, they have always reserved it for him."

"Have you ever seen the phantom, Madame?" Monsieur Moncharmin asked.

"No, but I have often heard his voice," Madame Giry replied. "He usually arrives in the middle of the first act. He gives three little taps on the door. He says that he is the phantom of the Opera House and that I must not be afraid."

The managers decided to investigate Box Five for themselves. It was silent in the huge and gloomy theatre. A few rays of eerie light shone onto the stage. In the gloom, they both saw a shape in the box. Neither of them spoke, but they stood for a while, staring until the figure had disappeared. When they went inside the box, there was nothing to be seen.

"Somebody is making a fool of us!" Monsieur Richard said. "We are showing the opera Faust again on Saturday evening. We shall both watch it from this box."

On the Saturday morning, the managers received another letter:

"My dear Managers

So it is to be war between us? If you still desire peace, you must give me back my private box and Christine Daaé must sing the part of Margarita tonight.

If you refuse, this Opera House will be cursed. Listen to my warning.

The Phantom of the Opera"

"I am sick of him!" Monsieur Richard cried, banging his fists upon the table.

As he spoke, the head groom of the Opera stables was shown in. The stables were in the cellars of the Opera. Here twelve horses were being trained for a procession in a forthcoming opera.

The groom was very agitated. "Cesar, the white horse, has been stolen," he explained. "There's no doubt in my mind who has done it. It was the phantom. I saw a black shadow riding a white horse that looked exactly like Cesar."

"And did you run after them?" Monsieur Richard asked.

"I did and I shouted," the groom replied, "but they were too fast for me. They disappeared."

Monsieur Richard stood up. "That is all," he said. "You can go." He smiled grimly. "We shall lodge a complaint against the phantom."

When the groom had left, Monsieur Richard turned to his colleague. "We must sack him at once," he said. "He'll tell his story of the phantom and everybody will be laughing at us. And we shall also sack Madame Giry."

Carlotta, who was to play the role of Margarita in Faust as usual that evening, was opening her morning letters. One was clumsily written in red ink: "If you sing tonight, you must be prepared for a great misfortune," she read, "a misfortune worse than death."

Carlotta had received such letters before, but never one quite as threatening as this.

"I shall sing the part of Margarita tonight even if I am dying," she said to herself.

A second letter arrived that evening. "If you are wise," it said, "you will realise that it is madness to try to sing tonight."

Carlotta took no notice of the threats. She sang the part of Margarita, while Christine Daaé took a smaller part. The first act of Faust passed without incident because Margarita did not appear in the first act. In the second act, Carlotta came onto the stage. The audience greeted her with great enthusiasm and applauded her more and more. Faust came onto the stage to join her. As he knelt on one knee to sing to her, Carlotta opened her mouth to sing with him – and she croaked like a toad.

The two managers in Box Five gasped in horror. They trembled as they felt the phantom all around them. They wanted to run away, but they dare not.

Carlotta croaked again.

"Sing!" Monsieur Richard called down to her.

Carlotta started the line again – and croaked.

The phantom was chuckling to himself in Box Five.

Then the managers heard his mouthless voice in their ears: "She is singing tonight to bring the chandelier down!"

They raised their eyes to the ceiling and uttered a terrible cry. The chandelier was slipping down towards them at the call of that fiendish voice. It smashed into the middle of the stalls amid a thousand shouts of terror.

Many people were wounded that night – and one woman was killed – the woman who had taken Madame Giry's job.

That tragic evening was bad for everybody. Although the verdict was accidental death caused by wear and tear of the chains that held the chandelier, the managers lost their confidence. And they gave Madame Giry back her job.

But something else happened that evening. Christine Daaé disappeared. And two weeks later, she was still missing.

CHAPTER FOUR

The Voice

Raoul was so worried about Christine that he came to the Opera House to ask the managers if they knew where she was.

"She requested a long leave of absence for reasons of health," Monsieur Moncharmin explained.

"Then she is ill!" he cried.

"We don't know," Monsieur Richard said. "She did not ask to see a doctor."

Raoul's thoughts were gloomy as he left the Opera for the house where Christine lodged with Madame Valerius. He knew that Christine had a vivid imagination and that she constantly brooded over her dead father. Music affected her a great deal.

"She will easily fall victim to a wicked person," he thought.

Madame Valerius received him kindly. "Monsieur de Chagny!" she cried. "I am pleased to see you! Now we can talk of Christine."

"But where is she, Madame?" Raoul asked.

"She is with her Angel of Music," the old lady replied. "She often talks of you, Raoul. She is fond of you, but you must know that she is not free to be with you."

"Why not?" he asked.

"The Angel of Music forbids her," Madame Valerius replied. "He tells her that she will never hear his voice again if she marries. She cannot live without her Angel. It was he played the violin at her father's grave."

"Madame," Raoul said. "How long has she known this angel?"

"About three months," she told him. "He began to give her lessons in her dressing-room at the Opera. But I do not know where she is having her lessons now."

Raoul left Madame Valerius angrily. "It is clear that she loves another man," he told himself.

He went straight to his brother's house and wept in his arms like a child.

"I must tell you that Christine Daaé was seen in the park last night in the company of a man," his brother said.

Raoul was very unhappy. That evening, he went to the park to watch for Christine! It was bitterly cold and the road was bright under the moonlight. Raoul waited. At last a carriage turned the corner of the road and came towards him. A woman leaned out in the pale moonlight.

"Christine!" Raoul cried.

Suddenly, the window closed and her face disappeared. The carriage rushed away. Raoul ran behind it calling Christine's name, but she did not reply. He stopped and stood in the silence, staring down that cold road. His heart was cold, too. She had not answered his cry.

***

The next morning, Raoul received a letter in a muddy, unstamped envelope.

"To the Viscount Raoul de Chagny: Go to the masked ball at the Opera the night after tomorrow," he read. "Wear a mask and a white hooded cloak. CHRISTINE"

"She must have thrown it from the carriage," Raoul thought, "in the hope that a passer-by would pick it up and deliver it."

"Whose prisoner is she?" he asked himself. "What monster has carried her off? And how has he done it? Of course! That man, whoever he is, has enchanted her with his music."

"I do not know whether to curse Christine or to pity her!" he thought. "I am inexperienced in love. Perhaps she is just making a fool of me."

The night of the ball came at last. Raoul felt ridiculous in his white cloak and mask trimmed with thick lace. But at least nobody would recognise him! Just before midnight, a figure in a black hooded cloak touched his hand briefly as he waited.

"Is that you, Christine?" he asked.

The person raised its fingers to its lips to warn him not to say the name again, and walked on. Raoul followed. He passed a group of people crowded around a man dressed in scarlet, a mask covering almost all his face.

"He is wearing the same mask as the man I saw in

Perros!" Raoul cried to Christine. "This time he shall not escape."

Christine pulled Raoul quickly into a private box and slammed the door.

"Who do you mean?" she asked.

"Who?" he asked angrily. "The man who hides behind that hideous mask, of course! Your friend, Madame … the Angel of Music! I shall snatch off his mask and we shall look each other in the face."

But Christine would not let him leave. "I came to tell you my secret this evening. But I cannot, not now that you have lost faith in me. Goodbye, Raoul. You shall not see me again." She walked away from him. "And do not follow me."

Raoul did not go after her, but when the ball was over, he made his way to Christine's dressing room. She was not there. Then, hearing footsteps outside, he hid behind a curtain. Christine came in. She flung her mask onto the table and he was shocked by the paleness of her face. "Poor Erik," she whispered.

She sat down at her table and began to write a letter. Suddenly she stopped and seemed to listen. The sound of singing came faintly through the walls. It was a man's voice, and it was beautiful. Christine stood up.

"Here I am, Erik," she said. "I am ready, but you are late."

Raoul peeped from behind the curtain. There was nobody else in the room. Christine's face had lit up, a smile of happiness on her bloodless lips. The voice went on singing a song from Romeo and Juliet…. "Fate links me to you for ever and a day!"

Christine stretched out her arms and began to walk towards the mirror, which covered one wall of her dressing room. Raoul came out of hiding and walked towards her. He put out his arms to embrace her, but as he did so an icy blast hit his face. He fell back, watching twenty images of Christine spinning around him.

When everything was still again, she had disappeared from the room that still echoed with singing.

CHAPTER FIVE

The Phantom of the Opera

The next day, Raoul was surprised to find Christine safely at home.

"There is a terrible mystery around you, Christine," he said, "a mystery much more dangerous than a phantom. Why will you not tell me where you have been for the last two weeks? You must allow me to protect you."

"I am the mistress of my own actions, Raoul," she replied angrily.

"You are under some sort of spell, Christine," he replied, "a very dangerous spell. You know there is no such person as the Angel of Music. Tell me, please! To whom does that voice belong? Who is Erik?"

Christine turned as white as a sheet.

"Raoul," she said. "Forget the man's voice. Do not even remember his name. You must never try to solve the mystery. Promise me."

Raoul promised. Then he left her, cursing Erik as he went.

***

Raoul was so unhappy that he decided to leave Paris.

"I shall be joining an expedition to the North Pole in a month's time," he told Christine. "Perhaps I shall die and never see you again."

"Perhaps I shall die, too," she replied.

To his surprise, the next few weeks were the happiest that Raoul had ever known. Christine took Carlotta's place as Margarita and she was a great success once more.

She also showed Raoul parts of the Opera House he had never seen, although she was always careful not to go too close to the trap doors in the stage. "Everything that is underground belongs to him!" she said, trembling.

But this happiness was spoilt by one thing – sometimes Christine disappeared for a day or two and she always returned unhappy and pale, her eyes red-rimmed. The day before he was due to leave Paris, Raoul could stand it no longer.

"I shall not go abroad until you tell me your secret," he said. "I want to remove you from Erik's power."

"Hush!" Christine said. "He may hear you. Follow me." She led him to the roof of the Opera House. The whole of Paris was spread out below them in the fine spring sunshine. They did not see the shape in the shadows behind them. "He is a devil, Raoul," she began. "He has allowed me this time to spend with you only because you are going away. Now we have only one day left. If I do not go back, he will fetch me with his voice. Then he will weep and tell me that he loves me."

"Let us go away from here today," Raoul replied.

"No," Christine said. "It would be too cruel! Let him hear me sing tomorrow evening. Then … then we can go away. I love you, Raoul." She sighed and trembled. "I feel that if I return to him again, I shall never come back."

"Tell me when you first saw him," Raoul said.

"The night when the chandelier fell," she replied. "The voice made me come to him. It was extraordinary, Raoul. My dressing room seemed to lengthen, and suddenly I was in a dark passage."

"You must have been dreaming," Raoul said.

"No," Christine replied. "A cold bony hand seized my wrist. I was in the hands of a man wrapped in a large cloak and wearing a mask that hid his face. I tried to scream, but he put his hand over my mouth. It smelt of death and I fainted. When I opened my eyes, he was splashing my face with water. Then he lifted me onto a white horse."

"Where did the horse take you?" Raoul asked.

"To the cellars of the Opera," Christine said. "We turned and turned downwards in a bluish light until we came to a boat fastened at the side of an underground lake. The man put me in it and rowed quickly across the water. He said: "Don't be afraid, Christine, you are in no danger." I tried to snatch away his mask. "You are in no danger as long as you do not see my face," he whispered. I cried and he knelt at my feet. "I am not an Angel, nor a phantom," he said. "I am Erik.""

"Christine, something tells me that it is wrong to wait until tomorrow evening," Raoul said. "We must leave now. Now that we know that Erik is not a phantom, we must speak to him." He paused. "Do you hate him, Christine?"

Christine shook her head. "How can I hate him, Raoul? He loves me! He has imprisoned me underground for love. He sang to me. I listened…and stayed. I was a prisoner in his house. But I had to know the face behind that voice." Christine shuddered. "Raoul, I pulled off his mask!"

Christine held Raoul's hand as she shivered violently.

"If I live to be a hundred, I shall still hear his cry of grief and anger when I saw that terrible sight! His face was like the face of a dead man, but it was alive! He had four black holes where his eyes, nose and mouth should be. I fell to my knees. "Feast your eyes!" he hissed at me. 'Look at

Erik's ugliness!" And when I turned away my head, he pulled me towards him with my hair."

"Enough!" Raoul cried. "Tell me where he is. I must kill him!"

"Oh, Raoul, listen," Christine continued. "He dragged me by my hair … it is too horrible … he seized my hands and dug them into his terrible flesh. "Now you have seen my hideous face, I cannot let you leave me." Christine looked at Raoul. "What more can I tell you, my dear?" she asked. "I stayed with him for two weeks. I lied about my feelings for him and he became my faithful slave. He even gained enough confidence to take me out. But that night you saw us in the park nearly caused my death. He was so jealous. But at last he let me go because I promised to go back."

"You say that you love me, but you went back!" Raoul groaned.

"Yes, my dear," she replied, "but not because I love him. It was because of the terrible cry he gave when I said goodbye. Poor Erik! Poor Erik!" She sighed. "I hoped my visits would calm him, but they make him mad with love for me."

Christine put her trembling arms around Raoul's neck. "I am so frightened, Raoul," she whispered, "so frightened."

The sky thundered as a storm approached. And as they ran from the roof, they saw two blazing eyes staring down at them.

CHAPTER SIX

Where is Christine?

Raoul returned home worried by all that he had just seen and heard.

"I shall save her from that terrible man," he said as he prepared to sleep that night. He blew out his candle. Two eyes, like blazing coals stared at him from the foot of his bed. Raoul was no coward but he trembled. He lit the candle and the eyes disappeared.

"Erik's eyes have disappeared in the dark but he may still be there," he thought.

Raoul looked around his room and under his bed like a child. Then he blew out the candle again. The eyes appeared outside his window. Raoul took his revolver and aimed a little above them.

The noise of the revolver brought his brother to his room. The count saw that there was a hole in the window at a man's height. Raoul was leaning over the balcony, laughing.

"Ah, there is blood!" he was saying. "That's good. A phantom that bleeds is less dangerous."

The count, thinking that Raoul was dreaming, shook him hard. "Have you gone mad?" he cried. "Wake up! You have shot a cat."

"That is quite possible," Raoul replied. "With Erik you never know."

"Who is Erik?" the count asked.

"He is my rival," Raoul said, "and if he's not dead that's a pity. But I shall take Christine Daaé away from him tonight."

***

At nine o'clock that evening, a carriage took its place outside the Opera House. Inside, the performance of Faust had begun. Christine did not sing well at first. Then Carlotta entered her box. She sneered at Christine and this sneer saved her. Christine wanted to triumph once more and she sang with all her heart and soul. In the last act, when she pleaded with the angels, she made all the members of the audience feel as if they, too, had wings.

Raoul stood up to face her and she stretched out her arms to him, singing: "My spirit longs to be with you."

Suddenly, the stage was plunged into darkness. When the gaslights were lit once more, Christine Daaé had disappeared. Raoul rushed onto the stage. Mad with despair, he called Christine's name and thought he heard her screams from the phantom's pit of darkness.

"Christine!" he shouted. "Are you alive?"

He ran to her dressing room. He wept before the mirror that had once let Christine pass to the darkness below, but the glass would not let him in.

When the police arrived, they asked to speak to Raoul in the managers' office. As he was entering the room, somebody whispered in his ear: "Erik's secrets must remain secret."

Raoul turned round. A man stood next to him, dark skinned with green eyes, his fingers on his lips.

"Is that monster your friend?" Raoul asked.

"Erik's secret is also Christine Daaé's secret," the man replied.

Then he bowed and walked away.

After speaking to the police, Raoul went to find the dark-skinned man again.

"You seem to know a lot," Raoul accused him impatiently, "but I do not have time to listen. I have to help Christine." He stared at the man, his face desperate. "What do you know, sir? Can you help me?"

CHAPTER SEVEN

Into the Cellars

The man turned and began to make his way towards Christine's dressing room. Raoul followed him. "I can try to take you to her … and to him," he said. "He may even be here now, in this wall, in this floor, in this ceiling. What did you tell the police?"

"That the phantom of the opera had abducted Christine," Raoul replied. "He did not believe me. He thought I was mad."

"We shall have to fight him," the man said. "You must be prepared for anything. This man is a dangerous enemy, more terrible than you can imagine. You love Christine Daaé, don't you?"

"I worship the ground she stands on," Raoul replied. "But why should you risk your life for her? Do you hate Erik?"

"No, sir," he said. "I do not hate him. If I did, I should have stopped him long ago. I have forgiven him the harm he has done me."

They entered the empty dressing room and the man walked over to the mirror. He pressed the wall around it.

"It is not a magic mirror," he explained. "It is on a

spring. But Erik may know already that we are coming after him. He may have cut the cords that turn it."

Suddenly, their reflection in the glass rippled. The mirror lit up and moved like a revolving door. It turned, carrying them from the light into the deep darkness. In the dim light of his companion's lantern, Raoul saw that they were in a narrow passage.

"We have only one way of helping Christine," the man said. "And that is to enter the house unseen. We can do that from the third cellar below this passage – at the exact spot where Joseph Buquet died."

They came to a light in the floor where they climbed down through a trap door into the third cellar. But there were too many people about – scene-shifters and policemen – so they hid for a while in the cellars below.

As they waited there, something moved in the darkness and a shining face without a body came towards them.

"I have never seen this before!" the man whispered to Raoul. "It is not Erik – he never comes down here – but it may be one of his tricks. Take care!"

They ran along the passage away from the head, but it followed them, with a sound like a thousand nails being scraped down a blackboard. The face was close now. Its eyes were large and staring, its nose crooked, its lower lip large and hanging.

They could go no further. Raoul and the man flattened

themselves against the wall at the end of the passage. Soon the face was level with them! Their hair stood on end in horror. Then they realised what the noise was. Rats! They climbed up the two men, biting and clawing them.

"Don't move! Don't move!" the face said. "You are quite safe. I am the rat-catcher. Just let me pass with my rats."

The rat-catcher walked on, dragging with him waves of scratching rats – and the two men breathed deeply again.

"We cannot be far from the underground lake down here," Raoul said. "Take me there now, please, sir."

"No, we cannot enter his house from the lake," his companion replied. "It is too well guarded. I myself was almost killed there."

"If you cannot help Christine, at least let me die trying to save her," Raoul said, hot with anger. "How can we enter his house without crossing the lake?"

"As I have already said, from the third cellar, sir," the man replied. "It is safe to return there now. And on our way back, I shall tell you how I first got to know Erik…"

CHAPTER EIGHT

The Persian's Story

"I first knew Erik in my own country, Persia," the man began. "He had had a sad life until then. He was born here in France, but his ugliness terrified his parents so much that he had run away from home. He had been shown in travelling fairs across Europe as a 'living corpse.' He learned the art of magic and music. He sang like nobody else – and he learned ventriloquism. You have heard how he made Carlotta croak. The Shah of Persia heard about him and invited him to come to his country to entertain him and his wife.

Erik was a very clever man. He built a palace full of tricks for the Shah, who was able to move about in it unseen and leave without anyone knowing. But the Shah did not want anybody else to have such a palace and he ordered Erik to be killed. I was the Chief of Police at that time and I helped Erik to escape.

I was forced to leave Persia and I came to live in Paris. Erik was tired of his life as a freak and he decided to live a normal life designing ordinary buildings. When this new Opera House was to be built in Paris, he was given the job of designing and building the foundations.

But when he found himself below the ground, his desire for the fantastic came back. He was an ugly freak. Why not build a house by the underground lake for his own use where he could hide from people's eyes for the rest of his life?

Poor, unhappy Erik! Shall we pity him or curse him? He only wanted to be like everybody else – but he was too ugly. With an ordinary face, he could have become a great man. Now he could only play tricks with his genius.

He could have had the world. Instead, he had to be happy with a cellar.

When Erik came to live permanently by the lake at the Opera House, I lived in fear of what he might do – although he told me that he had changed for the better. Whenever there was an accident, and everybody blamed the phantom, I suspected him. I often asked him to let me visit his house, but he always refused. I started to watch him all the time from the other side of the lake, to see how he entered his house. But I could not see properly in the darkness.

After that terrible night when the chandelier fell, I decided to talk to him. I rowed his boat across the lake to the wall where I had often seen Erik disappear into his house. Immediately, the silence was broken by the sound of singing. It rose from the waters of the lake. I leaned over the edge of the boat to listen, certain that this was another of Erik's tricks. Two arms seized my neck and began to drag me down into the water. I gave a cry. Erik recognised my voice. He did not drown me, but took me to the bank.

"Why do you try to enter my house?" he asked. "I did not invite you! Did you once save my life to make it unbearable?" He laughed horribly and showed me a long reed. "I can remain underwater for hours by using this to breathe. Now go and never come here again."

"What about the chandelier, Erik?" I asked.

He laughed again. And when Erik laughed he was more terrible than ever. Then he pushed off from the bank and disappeared into the darkness of the lake.

I continued to live in terror of what Erik might do to others at the Opera House. Whenever people talked about the phantom, I shivered – if only they knew that he really existed! He was a repulsive monster.

Yet his voice made Christine Daaé forgot his ugliness when he sang. I overheard him once in her dressing room. To my horror, I discovered his secret passage behind the mirror. When Christine disappeared for two weeks, I started to follow him – until I realised that he was following me! He warned me that if his secret was discovered, he would destroy many people.

"I am not looking for you, Erik," I explained, "but for Christine Daaé. You are keeping her a prisoner."

"You are wrong," he replied. "I am loved for my own

sake and I shall prove it to you. I shall let her come and go as she pleases."

"Prove it!" I said. "Then I shall leave you in peace."

"Very well," he said. "Christine will be at the masked ball tonight. And she will come back to me afterwards because she loves me. She will marry me. I have already written the music for our wedding."

To my astonishment, things have happened as he said they would. As you know, Christine keeps returning to his house. But I was still worried about her. The idea of another entrance to his house in the third cellar haunted me. I watched and waited in the shadows. One day, Erik came to scenery that was stored there. He pressed a spring that moved a stone in the wall. He passed through and it closed behind him.

I was too afraid to follow him that day. I could not forget that Joseph Buquet had died at that same spot – and I remembered Erik's warning. But I watched Christine closely. Erik filled her with terror, I could see that. She loved only you.

So, as you have seen my friend, I was prepared for action when Christine was abducted tonight. I shall rescue her – with your help, Monsieur de Chagny."

CHAPTER NINE

The Torture Chamber

At last, Raoul and the Persian reached the third cellar. Everybody had left now. They crawled along its floor until they came to the end wall. The Persian pressed the stones until one of them gave way. He wriggled through the hole and signalled for Raoul to follow him.

"There is a long drop!" he warned.

They slipped down quietly into a room below. Their lantern lit up a six cornered room with mirrors on every wall. An iron tree stood in one corner. It was reflected in every mirror so that they seemed to be in the middle of a forest. On the floor lay a rope.

"We are in Erik's torture chamber!" the Persian whispered. He paused to listen. "Ssh...! It's Erik!"

Erik's voice came from the other side of the wall. "You must make your choice, Christine," he said. "Do you want to hear the wedding mass or the funeral mass?"

Christine Daaé moaned at his words. Raoul wanted to break through the walls to free her.

"I can't go on living like a mole in the ground," Erik continued. "I want to live like everybody else. You will be the happiest of women, Christine. But you are crying! You are afraid of me. I am not wicked. If you loved me, I could be as gentle as a lamb."

Christine remained silent, but Erik began to cry in despair. Then a bell rang and they heard Erik slam the door as he left. At last, Christine was alone.

"Christine! Christine!" Raoul called. "We are here to save you! When you hear Erik return, warn us! We are in the torture chamber! Can you open the door to the house for us?"

"No, he has tied me up," Christine cried. "He has gone mad with love. He has decided to kill himself and everybody with him if I do not become his wife. I have until eleven o'clock tomorrow night to decide. The key to the door is in a leather bag," she sobbed. Christine struggled to free herself, but she could not. "Do not stay here!" she cried. "Erik is mad. Hush! I can hear him coming back."

"Remember that he loves you," the Persian said. "Smile at him and tell him that the ropes are hurting you."

The floor creaked on the other side of the wall and Christine gave a loud cry.

"I am in pain, Erik," she said. "Please loosen these ropes."

"Yes, I shall release you," he said. "I have had enough of this life, you know. You have only to refuse to marry me and it will be over for us all. You're free now … oh, my poor Christine! Look at your wrists. I have hurt them." He paused and cried out again. "That man who came to the door just now … he looked like … why, oh why did he come to my door? He is dead and I must sing a funeral mass for him…"

Erik began to sing and his voice surrounded them all, rising and falling like the sounds of a storm. Suddenly, he stopped. "What have you done with my bag, Christine?" he roared.

"I want to look at the room next door," she replied. "I have never seen it. I am a woman so I am curious."

"I do not like curious women," he shouted. "Now give the bag back to me!"

He laughed as Christine gave a cry of pain. Erik had obviously taken the bag from her. Raoul gave a cry, too.

"Did you hear that, Christine?" Erik asked. "It was a cry."

"No," she replied. "I cried out because you hurt me."

"You're lying!" Erik shouted. "There is somebody in the torture-chamber. The man you want to marry perhaps?" He laughed madly. "Well, we can soon find out, Christine. Climb those steps and peep in the little window up there. Tell me what he looks like."

"No! I'm frightened!" Christine cried. "I don't care about that room now."

"Go, dear," Erik replied.

Raoul and the Persian heard Christine's voice above their heads. "There is no one there, dear," she said. "Why do you call it the torture room, Erik? I can only see a beautiful forest."

Erik began to laugh. "It is a tropical forest!" he cried. I say woe to anybody who comes to look around my torture chamber. Ha! Ha! Ha!"

His mocking voice was everywhere. It passed through the walls. It passed between the Persian and Raoul.

"Stop, please, Erik!" Christine sobbed. "It is very hot up here. Yes, the wall is getting hot."

Erik went on laughing so hideously that Raoul banged on the wall like a madman himself. He heard a door slam on the other side. Then there was silence.

The torture chamber was getting hotter and hotter. As the heat became unbearable, Raoul walked up and down, calling Christine's name. The torture was beginning to work on his mind.

"We are in a magic room, that is all," the Persian said to calm him. "I know most of Erik's tricks. We shall leave the room as soon as we have found a way out. Please keep calm, sir, and let me find it."

The Persian touched the glass panels carefully, searching for a hidden spring. The heat was fierce and they were thirsty. As darkness fell, they heard the roar of a lion.

"It is only Erik," the Persian explained. "He has found a

way of imitating a lion's roar to perfection."

The forest began to change into a hot desert. As the time passed, they were beginning to die of heat and thirst.

"Look!" Raoul whispered. "There is an oasis ahead! And I can hear rain!"

"This is the worst of his tricks!" the Persian gasped. "He drops tiny pebbles into a box to imitate the patter of rain. If a man hopes for water and does not find it, he will hang himself from that tree. I am sure that is what happened to poor Joseph Buquet."

As they crawled around the room in despair, the Persian caught sight of a black-headed nail in the floor. He pressed it. Immediately, a cellar flap opened in the floor. They stumbled down a dark staircase into a cool room full of barrels. Taking out his knife, the Persian worked hard to open one of them.

"This isn't water," Raoul cried out. "It's gunpowder!"

CHAPTER TEN

The Scorpion or the Grasshopper?

Raoul and the Persian remembered Erik's words to Christine. "He has decided to kill himself and everybody with him if I do not become his wife." She had until eleven o'clock to decide. Erik had chosen his time well. The Opera House would be full of people then.

A terrible thought came into the Persian's mind. How long had they been imprisoned in the torture chamber? Terrified, they climbed back to the chamber, calling out to Christine.

"What time is it?" they asked.

At last, she answered them. "Five minutes to eleven," she replied, "the hour that is to decide life or death." Christine started to sob with relief. She had not expected to find Raoul still alive. "Erik has torn off his mask!" she cried. "He is completely mad. He has given me the bronze key from his bag, which opens two ivory boxes. In one is a bronze scorpion. If I turn it round, that means yes and I shall have to marry him. In the other is a bronze grasshopper. That means no, and he will blow us all up. He has left to give me these last five minutes to decide."

"Christine," the Persian cried. "Where are you?"

"Standing by the scorpion," she replied.

"Don't touch it!" he shouted. "Erik may have deceived you again. Perhaps it is the scorpion that will blow us to pieces. Perhaps he has escaped and left us to die."

But soon they heard Erik's footsteps.

"Erik!" the Persian called out. "You know who I am, don't you?"

"So you are not dead, my friend?" Erik replied. "Not a word from you or I shall blow everything up. Now listen, Christine! If you turn the grasshopper, we shall all be blown to pieces. But if you turn the scorpion, I shall release water to soak the gunpowder. I promise. You have two minutes to decide."

A terrible silence fell. Raoul knelt down and began to pray.

"Erik!" Christine said at last. "I have turned the scorpion!"

Raoul and the Persian felt a rumble beneath their feet. Then they heard the hiss of water. They looked down. The barrels were covered with water, and they both drank deeply. But to their horror, the water continued to rise.

"Turn off the scorpion now, Erik!" they shouted. "That is enough water to soak the gunpowder!"

But there was no reply from the next room. They were alone in the swirling water, hanging onto the iron tree. And the water rose higher.

"Erik!" the Persian cried out. "Remember, I saved your

life once!"

They began to swim to find a way out, but they quickly lost their strength. Then they swirled round and round, until they sank under the dark water….

***

When the Persian opened his eyes again a few days later, he was in his own house. He learned from his servants that Raoul had not been seen in Paris. An even greater tragedy had happened. Raoul's brother's body had been found on the bank of the lake under the Opera House.

"There is no doubt in my mind that the poor count had been trying to find his brother," he thought. "He was the visitor who rang the bell that day we were in the torture chamber."

His servant announced the arrival of a stranger who would not give his name. A man, hidden by a large cloak and hat, was shown into his room.

He looked very weak and leaned against the wall. Taking off his hat, he revealed his ghostly mask.

It was Erik.

"You have murdered Count Philippe!" the Persian cried. "What have you done with his brother and Christine Daaé?"

Erik sighed. "It was an accident," he gasped. "Count Philippe was already dead by the time I left my house … he fell into the water … I have come here … to tell you … that I am going … to die … I am dying of love …"

"Is she dead or alive?" the Persian asked, shaking Erik's arm.

"No, no, she is not dead," Erik replied. "She saved your life. You were drowning. Christine came to me with her beautiful blue eyes and begged me to stop the water. Half a minute later, it was all back in the lake."

"What have you done with Raoul de Chagny?" he cried.

"He was my hostage for a while," Erik replied. "I locked him up in the fifth cellar where nobody ever goes. Christine was waiting for me. A real and living bride … and I kissed her … my mother would never let me kiss her! She used to run away from me … and throw me my mask! No other woman has ever kissed me … I fell at Christine's feet … she cried!" Erik sobbed out aloud. "I tore off my mask to feel her tears on my face. She did not run away. We cried together. I have tasted happiness at last!" Erik fell onto a chair, choking for breath. "She took my hand … I gave her a golden ring as a wedding present for her … and Raoul." Erik stopped. "I am choking. I must take off my mask. Do not look at me."

The Persian went to look through the window, his heart full of pity for Erik.

"I released the young man," Erik continued, "and told him to come with me to Christine. I made Christine promise to come back when I was dead and bury me in secret … I told her

where to find my body. Then Christine kissed me for the first time, here on the forehead … no, don't look! Then they left together, to find a priest in some lonely place to marry them."

The Persian asked him no more questions. No one could have doubted the word of the weeping Erik that night. The monster put on his mask again.

"Just before I die," he said, "I shall send you the belongings that Christine left behind – a pair of gloves, a shoe-buckle and two handkerchiefs. When you receive them, please put an announcement of my death in the newspaper for her to read."

That was all. Erik left and went out to a waiting carriage.

"Take me to the Opera House," he told the driver.

Three weeks later, the Paris newspaper carried this announcement: ERIK IS DEAD.

Epilogue

During building work at the Opera House thirty years later, a skeleton was found. It was in the place where Erik had first held the fainting Christine in his arms before he carried her down to his house on the lake.

On its finger was a gold wedding ring.

Glossary

Key:

adj	adjective
adv	adverb
n	noun
phr	phrase
phr v	phrasal verb
(superl)	superlative
vi	intransitive verb
vt	transitive verb

abduct, to	*vt*	to kidnap	31
back-stage	*n*	the area behind the stage where the dressing rooms, scenery etc. are	6
ball	*n*	a formal event with dancing	19
blast	*n*	a rush of wind	7
box	*n*	a small, private area at a theatre, like a balcony, where people sit to watch the performance	5
brood over, to	*phr*	to think about something a lot in a way that makes you unhappy	17
carry off, to	*phr v*	to remove	19
chandelier	*n*	a large glass light fitting with lots of individual lights	16
cloak	*n*	a kind of large coat without sleeves	19

clumsily	*adv*	not carefully	15
cord	*n*	a rope	32
coward	*n*	a person who is not brave	7
croak, to	*vi*	to make noise like a frog	15
crooked	*adj*	not straight	32
curse, to	*vt*	if you curse a place, you say that you will make bad things happen there	14
deformed	*adj*	if something is deformed, it doesn't have its usual shape	4
distinguished	*adj*	noble; very successful	5
eerie	*adj*	very strange and frightening	13
embrace, to	*vt*	to put your arms around someone with affection	22
enchant, to	*vt*	if someone enchants you, they make you feel great pleasure	4
expedition	*n*	a journey made for a particular purpose, for example to explore a region	24
faithful	*adj*	if you are faithful to someone, you are loyal to them and stay with them	27
fate	*n*	your fate is what you believe will happen to you, which you cannot control or influence; destiny	21
fiendish	*adj*	devilish	16

flap	*n*	a small door, like a trap door	42
forthcoming	*adj*	which will happen soon	14
freak	*n*	a person who is very strange or not normal	34
genius	*n*	great intelligence	35
grief	*n*	very great sadness	26
grimly	*n*	with a sad or serious expression	14
groom	*n*	a person who looks after horses	14
hideous	*adj*	very ugly	21
hostage	*n*	a person who has been kidnapped	46
inherit, to	*v t*	if you inherit money, somebody leaves you money when they die	4
inn *(old fashioned)*	*n*	a pub with rooms where you can sleep	9
ivory	*n*	the white, bone-like material that comes from elephants' tusks	43
leave of absence	*phr*	permission to be away from your job	17
misfortune	*n*	something very unpleasant or unlucky	15
mistress of one's own action	*phr*	responsible for what you do (used for women)	23
mocking	*adj*	which makes fun of someone	41
Monsieur	*n*	a French term of address which means 'Sir'	8

obsessed	*adj*	if you are obsessed with someone, you think about them all the time	4
passer-by	*n*	a person who is walking past	19
peasant	*n*	a farmer who works on a small area of land	8
phantom	*n*	a ghost	4
plead, to	*vi*	to beg; to ask insistently	29
red-rimmed	adj	with a red border all around	24
reed	*n*	a type of plant with long thin stems that grows in water	36
repulsive	*adj*	horrible and disgusting	36
rival	*n*	a competitor; a person who wants the same things as you do	29
row, to	*vi*	to make a boat move using an oar (a long piece of wood)	25
rowdiness	*n*	noisy behaviour	12
rumour	*n*	something that people are saying but which may not be true	12
scarlet	*adj*	bright red	20
scenery	*n*	the large painted panels used on the stage in the theatre	7
scene-shifter	*n*	a person who works in a theatre, changing the scenery	6
scrape, to	*vt*	to drag one thing over another	32

sneer, to	*vi*	to say something or use a facial expression that shows you do not respect someone	29
spine-chilling	*adj*	very frightening	4
stalls	*pl n*	the seats on the ground floor of a theatre	16
stretcher	*n*	a stretcher is used to carry sick or injured people and is made from strong material with a pole down each side	7
torture chamber	*n*	a room where people are tortured (hurt repeatedly, physically or mentally)	38
trap door	*n*	a small opening in the floor of a stage	24
trimmed	*adj*	decorated; edged	19
ventriloquism	*n*	the art of speaking without moving your lips	34
verdict	*n*	an official decision	16
vivid	*adj*	a vivid imagination is a very active and creative one	17
wear and tear	*phr*	the general, gradual damage to something caused simply by using it	16

The Phantom of the Opera Test Yourself

Exercise 1

Answer these questions.

1 Why did Christine Daaé replace Carlotta as Margarita in Faust?

2 Why was Raoul surprised to see Christine in the opera?

3 Where did Christine come from?

4 According to Christine, what was the voice in her dressing room?

5 Who were Monsieur Richard and Monsieur Moncharmin?

6 What happened when Carlotta tried to sing the part of Margarita?

7 What did Christine ask Raoul to wear at the masked ball?

8 What did Christine do when she heard the singing in her dressing room?

9 Where did Christine go on the white horse?

10 What did Christine see when she pulled off Erik's mask?

Exercise 2

Are these sentences true (T) or false (F)?

1   Raoul saw two eyes outside his window and shot just above them.

2   Christine rushed off the stage because she was not singing well.

3   The Persian hates Erik.

4   Raoul and the Persian saw a rat-catcher in the passage underneath the Opera House.

5   Erik was born in Persia.

6   Erik used a long reed to drag the Persian under the water.

7   The torture-chamber gradually became hotter and hotter.

8   The Persian pressed a black-headed nail and opened a secret door in the torture-chamber's roof.

9   The bronze scorpion released water to soak the gunpowder.

10 Erik killed Raoul's brother.

Answers

1 because Carlotta was ill

2 because he used to play on the beach with her when they were children

3 Sweden

4 the Angel of Music

5 the new managers at the Opera House

6 she croaked like a toad

7 a white hooded cloak and a mask

8 she walked towards her mirror and disappeared

9 to the cellars of the Opera House

10 four black holes where his eyes, nose and mouth should be

1 T; 2 F; 3 F; 4 T; 5 F; 6 F; 7 T; 8 F; 9 T; 10 T